I0543548

Foolish Wager and Other Stories

A.K. Harlan

Other works by A.K. Harlan

Collected Stories
Collected Stories II
Journey

Dedicated to those who have always been there for me

By the Light of the Moon

My son's name was Lonnie and by an early age he began showing signs of Hypertrichosis or Werewolf's Syndrome. By the age of 16 he was diagnosed with generalized Hypertrichosis. In other words, this rare condition causes excessive hair growth anywhere on the body. In Lonnie's case it is his entire body.

As the hair on his face and hands began to appear, he was no longer comfortable being seen by anyone except his family. He became obsessed in watching old Werewolf movies.

When Lonnie began to growl rather than speak, we were at a loss of what to do with this child. The boy began sitting in the front yard in the evenings waiting, watching for a full moon. He disclosed that he thought of this, and it was all he looked forward to seeing.

His school friends would stop by to check on him, but he only shook his head in refusal. The last words he spoke to us were "waiting for the full moon and you will then see what this is all about." As there is no cure for his illness we merely said we would be with him when the autumn moon was full and bright.

It is not as though we did not attempt to treat the condition, but electrolysis failed, and it has the best results, yet his hair just continued to grow back. The day arrived and he slept in that morning not wishing to be home schooled on this special occasion.

Lonnie had been practicing howling for days. In the evening, we all gathered in the front yard to get a good view of the moon. As the clouds parted exposing the lovely moon, Lonnie howled, lunged at his brother, bit him then ran haphazardly down the road. Neighbors witnessing this called the police. They tried to stop him by calling out that they only wanted help. With that he dove for the officer named Basil then with that the other Officer Silver sent a bullet into my son's heart ending his nightmare. May he rest in peace.

In the Blink of an Eye

To begin to tell you of my brother's life I must say that he has LiS-locked in syndrome. This is a neurological disorder that paralyzed almost all of his voluntary muscles, while preserving eye movement and blinks. This was caused by damage to the brainstem's pons, which contains nerve fibers that relay information to other parts of the brain.

Like Jean-Dominique Bauby, we hope he will be able to communicate through eye movement or blinking. Bauby's LiS was the result of a stroke. My brother sustained his injury at 26 while skiing a tough slope in Chamonix-Mont-Blanc which is a spot near the junction of France, Switzerland and Italy. After the Winter Olympics in 1924 it quickly developed into one of the world's first and best-known ski resorts. It has retained this celebrity.

It is no wonder Jeff chose to go there. As soon as I saw him and realized the extent of his injury, I sought help. Bauby's book The Diving Bell and the Butterfly gave me hope that after much work it will be possible for my brother to communicate again. It will be a process. A process of trial and error and requiring the utmost patience.

As Jeff would want and expect, I am up to the task of this painstaking process.

We will follow Bauby's example going through the alphabet. He will blink for the letter he wants. A few years have now passed and today he blinked for the assistant to transcribe, "Thank you, my sister."

Determined

This yarn is actually biographical. Upon telling the story to a friend, I thought I would write about it.

As a 13-year-old, I was energetic and adventurous. It was my first year of Junior High School and I became friends with a girl in my homeroom. She lived adjacent to the school.

Our friendship grew and by our second year we were visiting at one another's houses. Lynn's street was very steep, it met up with Grinstead Drive, a busy thoroughfare.

Lynn and I became friends with a boy in the grade behind us. He was cute, and funny and nice to be with. To add to this, he had a brother living in oh-so exotic California,

We would meet up at Lynn's house and "sidewalk surf" on madras skateboards, we designed and built. The summer vacation began in June, and we were ready.
Then to top it all off, Robin joined us with a skateboard his brother had gotten for him in San Francisco.

He declared he would give each of us a turn. I campaigned to go next and won. I ran to the top of the street, jumped aboard and flew down the street towards Grinstead Drive.

Toward the bottom, I realized I was not going to be able to stop before going into the road. So, instinctually I jumped off. We watched as the wonderful skateboard went down the sewer.

5

This dilemma did not deter me, I told Robin and Lynn to take hold of my hands and lower me down. When I felt something beneath my bare feet, I thought it was a metal bar but no, it was the skateboard. It floated!!

Somewhat like a monkey, I was able to secure the board between my feet., yelled bring me up and the day was saved.

The Columbarium

It was 4:30 and I knew the cemetery would close at 4:45. Hurrying in the door of the columbarium, it closed snuggly behind me. Nothing came to mind when I heard the lock click. Being my first time here it was interesting to look at the ornamental urns placed carefully in their niches.

I sought the urn which contains the cremains of my dear neighbor, Margaret. Kneeling to the floor in front of her, I said a little prayer ending with the sign of the cross. She would like that.

Feeling immensely sad at the prospect of life without my confessor, I rose and turned to go. As my hand clasped the handle it did not give; I was locked in, and the cemetery is now closed. Feeling rather panicky, I realized that there was nothing to do but settle in for the night.

Removing my jacket and placing it like a pillow beneath my head, I stretched out hoping sleep would come quickly. Sleep came slowly, but finally slumber enveloped me. Yet as I drifted off my name was uttered in a hauntingly familiar voice. Looking to the urn I saw what can only be described as a white mist emanating from the top of the urn containing Margaret.

It had no form just a wispy apparition. Softly inquiring "Margaret, is that you?" It was just a feeling, but I was convinced this was my deceased neighbor. The image floated towards me, pressing against me yet I felt nothing. A sense of awareness overtook me and a feeling of fear or apprehension. Believing that was a warning of impending doom, I cowered in the corner as the mist began to fade back towards the urn. In the morning light, I shook off all feelings of dread and awaited my release by one of the cemetery guards. I expected a good scolding.

To this day the belief that my encounter was a warning I have since then used caution in every walk of life. After a few years. I relaxed and when my boss asked me to take United Airline Flight 93 from Newark to San Francisco I was eager to go. I will have a meeting with the parent company, issue resolved and I will return home. Yes, life is good.

Delving

To explain an interest in "Delving" into someone's thoughts implies attempting to understand or explore their inner mental state. This could involve trying to guess their feelings, motivations, or beliefs, observing their behavior, expressions or indirectly through psychological research. Well, the conclusion to be reached here is yes, indulge yourself and delve into the thoughts of the Mad Monk, Rasputin.

A little background before trying to summons his thoughts, we will peer inside his brain. Grigori Rasputin was born in 1869, he was a Siberian peasant turned mystic, who rose to prominence in the Russian court due to his alleged ability to soothe the hemophiliac heir to the throne, Alexi.

So let the mystery of Rasputin's mind begin to unfold. He had an early life of destitution which may have led to a religious epiphany. He spent time in a monastery but was never formally ordained. This epiphany could have been caused by a lack of food due to poverty. He had his sights set on greater accomplishments.

His reputation grew as a healer and spiritual advisor. It was his influence on the royal family that led to his introduction to court. He realized he was receiving both admiration and resentment. By this time, he had begun to believe in his mysticism. The talk of his licentiousness left him unbothered. He brooded that the public image of him as being a dangerous influence stemmed from jealousy.

Finally, all this amounted to his assassination in 1916. He was poisoned, shot and ultimately drowned in the Neva River. Gaze at any available photo of him; the eyes that mesmerize that can never be fully understood. Did he believe in this aura, his influence on Alexandra Romanoff. All this ends with Rasputin' s body floating in the river.

Cotard's Delusion

My husband has Cotard's Delusion or Cotard's Syndrome. Its cause is unknown. There are speculations as to its etymology. Some suggest it is neurological, while others believe it is a psychiatric condition including severe depression, schizophrenia, or a brain injury.

This state is also known as walking corpse syndrome. I know it is a rare condition characterized by delusions of being dead or non-existent. Luke believes he is dead.

This began about a year ago. He would lie in a corpse-like position, in the morning never replying when I asked him if he was going to get out of bed. Finally, it came to a point when threats, pleading, and crying fell on deaf ears.

Now to a rational or questioning human, it would naturally occur that there are technical aspects to the situation. Incontinence and lack of food. He seems to attend to his bodily needs. Then one morning, I saw him walking in the hall and the walking dead was an appropriate description. Slow, plodding movements, it broke my heart.

Our house became a tomb, and time was doled out by how many empty cat food cans accumulated. I was not a practicing Christian, but I did know some Biblical lore. And I fervently wished, like Lazarus, he would rise from the dead.

11

It has never been determined what caused this onset. I believe it is severe depression. He had recently lost his parents in an auto accident. He spiraled downward with shock.

His friend Peter stopped by to see him. They had been close, and he was greatly affected by his friend's condition. Another visitor was Paul, an old friend dismayed by the words from the doctor which I relayed to him.

Thus began a treatment of neuroleptics for him in the event his case was truly schizophrenia. There was no change or reaction. All along I believed it was severe depression due to his parents fatal accident.

Then began treatment with Seroquel.

I had begun a regimen of physical therapy with him to work out his atrophying limbs. There was hope. Then after one exercise he grasped my hand. His eyes had a new light, a new expression, and color began to return to his cheeks. Within a few more weeks he croaked out "I love you." I knew, he was back.

Plans for the future? Take one day at a time. There will be therapy sessions, a normal diet, gradual walks.

Homicidal Eyes

Everyone liked Lucy, her kind winning smile and gentle nature charmed all that met her. It was noted that she and her husband moved around the nation considerably, but all thought there are some that cannot stay in one place.

Slowly, her malicious side began to surface, and it was puzzling to see how her behavior could change so rapidly. In a conversation about a local, unpopular politician, the truth won out. This man, it was believed, brought his 4-year-old son to public meetings for self-protection. After all, who would harm a man with his little son present and at his side.

She said brutally, "I would shoot through the kid to get to him." This comment was laughed off but left a lasting impression. It was that, and the expression in her eyes that caused actual fear in her acquaintances.

It came as no surprise then, when they found she had been arrested for a string of murders she had committed over the years. In the five other states she had lived in, a babysitter, a nurse, a postman, a dentist and a teacher had all been brutally killed.

It was due to her offhand comment that one of the people present decided to look into her background, researching the various states. Lucy had supplied them with the information as to where she had lived believing no one would associate her with the heinous crimes.

While in custody, she tipped her hand when the accuser was mentioned and the look on her face and in her eyes was positively murderous. She was given a choice of lethal injection or electric chair.

Fostered

Josie was a tall girl and very slender. At the time of our meeting, she was 18. She was happy for the most part or I believed she was, I never gave it much thought.

She had been in and out of foster homes since the age of 7and her file said, "no longer eligible for adoption." She can only stay with a foster family for a total of 5 months, after that she becomes uncontrollable.

I am a social worker, and her case came to my attention as a final resort. I work with the troubled children. When foster children turn 18, they "age out" of the system and become legal adults, meaning they are no longer considered a child under the law and foster care service ends. In some states the age is 21, but not here.

The scariest part involving Josie is the fact that one in every 5 fostered youth is homeless when they age out at 18. Ten percent of foster children are placed in institutions or group homes. I work in one of the group homes.

We are located in a small Kentucky town and the duplex has 4 residents in each apartment, and one has a recent vacancy so there is a place for Josie. She was transitioned a week after her 18th birthday. Already residing at the home was Luke, Michael and Essie May. Luke was capable of working a part-time job at the local grocery as a bagger.

Josie was considered stable enough to also work at the grocery as a bagger. Luke had told her about a possible position. She was anxious to be hired and was successful after the interview. But then after 5 months everything changed.

Josie, in a rage, threw the contents of a lady's grocery bag to the floor and berated the woman. Not only was the girl fired but she was incarcerated in an institution. Her future is not bright, she will no doubt spend the rest of her life institutionalized.

Collective Consciousness

This refers to the shared beliefs, ideas, values and norms that unify a society or group, acting as "social glue" and shaping individual cohesion. This "social glue" was pressed upon the group, or cult actually. There have been four notorious cults in American history. The term "cult" is controversial. The word is often used to describe belief systems that many consider "weird". It is generally used to describe a group with a leader that has a dangerous amount of control over his followers.

First comes to mind, Jim Jones the leader of the People's Temple. He led a mass suicide of over 900 Americans. Second, is the well-known Manson Family where Charles Manson projected himself as a religious figure in order to persuade young women to "follow him." This resulted in the Sharon Tate murders. His wishes were carried out in brutal fashion. Third, is Heaven's Gate. This group was led by Marshall Applewhite and Bonnie Lu Nettles. On their spiritual journey together they believed that God, Jesus and angels were extraterrestrials. In March of 1997 he and his followers took a lethal mixture of phenobarbital and vodka and wrapped their heads in plastic bags. All were found with a $5 bill and rolls of quarters in their pockets; each were wearing the same Nike shoes. They pushed their beliefs about their theories on their website before the mass suicide. Fourth The Branch Davidian all believed that the messiah was yet to come. In 1981 David Koresh joined the group who believed he was the Messiah. He went on to father 13 children by many women most of whom were underage. On April 19,1993 the FBI raided the compound

Koresh had established and a fire broke out killing 76 of the 85 Branch Davidian members. Koresh was among the dead.

Fueled by information about forming these cults, self-named Moses Green formed his cult following with what he called a vision of the future. He attracted both men and women and as he was wealthy, he supplied them with food and shelter. In order to become a member, the individual must kill a child so it would not live into the future; a future that he predicted would be violent and an uncontrollable society. They were to drink the blood of the innocent child; thereby, attaining an innocence they had lost. As word spread of this cult the authorities were shocked into action. Before they could intervene, all the 100 members cut their wrists simultaneously and all the FBI found were their lifeless bodies. It became a legend, and children were warned not to follow in the cult leader's footsteps.

Pandemonium

That was how she described her thoughts; as her mind was in ultimate chaos. It overtook her gradually as she was thrown into a state of disorder or uproar. She was horribly affected by the daily news. It led to depression and thoughts of suicide which her faith would not allow.

Barely a day passed that she was not assaulted by articles she read in the newspaper. She consulted a doctor with these fears and was told to avoid any type of happenings in the world. However, she could not stop herself; she felt at all times that she had to know what was going on.

Church was no help nor was the spiritual group she sought out for comfort. They seemed to rely on one another to share what they called the horror of existence. They all came to the conclusion that there was nothing to be done to improve their lives. So, as is said "misery loves company." What was to be done? They knew, like their newest member, that a mass suicide was out of the question. One of the group came up with what all considered an excellent solution.

It was decided that they would kill each other. Everyone purchased a handgun and the plan was fomented. The creator of this solution said he would be the last to go and had no fear of killing himself. They met in an open field and the deed was done leaving all who heard the news puzzled as they left no reason for their actions. Case closed.

No Regrets

As a devout Christian Mary often sought to rehabilitate criminals with religion. She truly believed in the Bible and the teachings of Christ. In her quest, she became involved with a man already incarcerated. It began innocently enough through shared letters.

The correspondence continues several years despite her knowing he was a mass murderer. He often asked her to come to the prison for a visit. He could be charming, and they began to plan for her to pay him a call.

Upon their first meeting, she was struck by how handsome he was. She rather ashamedly admitted to herself that he was sexy, and her mind wandered to the possibility of a conjugal visit. This contradicted her religious bent, but she dismissed it.

Years after their first encounter it was decided by officials that they could wed, and the ceremony was planned. At last, they could meet without the glass enclosure keeping them apart. When the visit was finally granted, both were beside themselves with excitement. Mary would meet with him at the prison.
In time, this California prison allowed her to have an unsupervised conjugal visit. Unfortunately, all did not go well. When Mary had completed the Bible session with him, pushing him to be a better person; he killed her.*

As he was already imprisoned without parole, nothing changed for him, and it was recorded in his file that he showed no regret whatsoever. He claimed he did it in God's name.

* This story is loosely based on an actual case that occurred in 1993, California does not recognize capital punishment. This is not uncommon as several similar cases have occurred over the years.

Her Perspective

This is my story; the story of one pushed to performing an act of desperation. I am a nurse working in the newborn's floor at a hospital in Chicago. Twins have been born, and it is time for me to help myself. No one needs two babies at once, so one will be liberated from the confines of being a twin.

It is just a matter of when and I will have to act fast. The twin baby will be taken just as I leave the evening shift. Arrangements have been made. The family is expecting a newborn baby boy tonight. And I will deliver.

Being aware that generally it is not recommended giving newborns any sleep medication. I will give him a low dose of melatonin. This will ensure a quiet departure.

If a huge debt had not been incurred by school loans and just being able to make ends meet, I would not have the need for immediate action. Now the deed is done. The meeting place has been selected, and we will meet at midnight.

I will hand over the infant and then receive the $25,000 I need to get out of debt. May God forgive me.

This story is based on the Paul Froncza story of a twin that was kidnapped at birth. DNA testing revealed he had a brother who had died the year of his discovery. They never met.

22

The Ambiverts

If was one of those times, she sought solitude. She wanted to sit quietly and dissect the evenings conversations. The introvert within her felt she could finally be alone. Enjoying an evening of social interactions, she discussed travel plans and learning where other's journeys had taken them. But once alone she no longer felt the exhilaration of being with others. She retreated into a time of self-awareness.

Recent research she conducted, revealed that introversion is a personality trait characterized by a focus on internal feelings rather than an external sense of stimulation.

Friends and family members noticed her mood swings and urged her to see someone about them. They felt she was bi-polar. She refused to discuss the symptoms with anyone, much less a doctor. Yes, there were times when tending to be quieter and more reserved, she would become introspective.

The woman was reluctant to call Ambiverts Anonymous but decided it best to delve into the possibilities she could live a more stable existence by sharing her experiences with others. In true eccentric style, the attendees were blindfolded and made to sign a release from any responsibility for the actions of the members of the group. The contract was drawn up by people hosting the meeting.

They meet on Fridays, and she found she looked forward to the meetings. The stories were varied, and it was such an odd mix as many were in the extrovert phase while others were in the introvert phase. There were those chatting everyone up, while others were already making excuses to leave as they found it all a bad idea.

There was one voice, well-spoken and gentle that intrigues her. Interestingly they both started out as extroverts but by the end of the evening, they only longed for isolation. Their seeking seclusion was shared verbally at the meeting's end. Surprised, they faced one another, removed the blindfolds and shared a smile. He took her hand in his and they walked to her car. Few words were spoken as if there was a silent agreement not to destroy the moment.

He never returned to the meetings, nor did she. They often thought of one another but could just not take the initiative to try to make contact. They lived in the same town, attended many of the same activities, yet their paths never crossed again.

Unsettling

Her life was pretty simple. She had a job she liked, for the most part. Trying to change to keep up with technology was not her strong suit. There were younger friends who would recommend she catch up to the times. They said she should stream and get a smart phone as well as subscribe to a music channel.

A close friend, her age, with younger children was also being guided into the modern age of the 21st century. The two would share information when they Facetimed. One of those days, her friend suggested she get rid of all her C.D.s she had long ago shed her albums. So, she did, and was told to get an Amazon Echo Show.

She didn't hesitate, it was ordered and delivered within days. At this time an old love interest had entered her life, and she became moon-eyed and thought of little else. It was then she began requesting Echo play the Loggins and Messina's work , A Love Song.

As night approached, she requested her usual song and was answered by silence, then a voice emitting from the speaker said, "Why don't you #### off?" Shocked, she unplugged the machine and left it like that overnight. The next day, she thought, "don't be silly," and plugged it back in. She never asked to hear "A Love Song" again.

The Severn River

It was on a trip to her mother's in Maryland when she discovered that her cousin Joseph was still going to be there. She had known him since childhood as he lived in a small Belgian village, Henri Chapelle, near the town of Welkenraedt where her grandparents lived.

Enough on the background of their relationship though in total she had been in his presence only a few times over the years. There was 16 years difference in their ages. He was the senior, and newly divorced. She was seeking respite from her severely depressed husband who she finally realized she could not "cheer up."

Fall had arrived and the drives in the area were good for the soul. She suggested they go down to the river and they hopped into her mother's yellow Toyota and and headed in the river's direction. Upon arrival, they parked and sauntered toward the water framed by colorful woods.

While they enjoyed the scene, two men approached them from the trees. They looked to be in their mid-forties and out of shape. The smaller man's hands shook as he advanced toward them holding a knife. Her cousin turned to her and quietly said "run." With that she exclaimed to the two men "look at that, there's a snake by your feet. A big snake. It's gonna get you." She turned looked at Joseph and said, "Come on Joseph." They walked to the car, got in and drove away.

They never spoke about this to one another or anyone, and Joseph never looked at her the same way.

Life or Death

At middle-age he was convinced that he had died in his sleep or from Ondine's Curse. He decided not to tell anyone of his death as he thought it quite unusual that he could still function. He was treated no differently by his family and close friends. He concluded that he could take risks as the worst had already happened.

The day had been a busying one and he grew physically tired which he also found compelling. He reasoned that he should not feel anything at all. Lying back in the recliner, he distractedly chose a nearby magazine to peruse.

As he flicked through the pages an article suddenly leapt out at him from Psychology Today. Do You Think You Are Dead? the title screamed at him. He discovered that there is a delusion known as Cotard's Syndrome in which an individual believes he is dead.

Feeling jubilant and immensely relieved that he was indeed still living, he rushed out the door to share his news. Jumping into his car, he paid no attention backing out of the driveway and was struck and killed by a speeding truck.

Everyone agreed that the last few months of his life had passed in a bizarre manner agreeing that often he would make inexplicable comments. They never knew or even guessed his condition.

A Cryptic Oddity

That is what he called her, C.O. or CoCo. He found her enchanting yet puzzling. He told her that he did not mean codependent although she had her doubts. As he would remind himself, "she is a walking contradiction."

She was outspoken, yet timid. She liked to say that she cultivated her eccentricities. Life was a challenge for her, one which she gladly accepted.
Then the depression would start.

She had auditory hallucinations such as hearing a voice loudly exclaiming "Jay zus." She was finally told by a therapist that this is long distance listening. This did nothing to reassure her, but she did enjoy knowing others underwent this as well. She decided she must research this.

She hid her depression by being mysterious and unavailable. She was always ready with an excuse for why she was incommunicado. Not talking about it, not dealing with it made it less a reality, but that cure never lasted long.

He had no notion of her suicide attempts and stays in a mental hospital. These disappearances only wetted his curiosity. He too had he's eccentricities and strove to practice "body in the flow" or a state of intense concentration. He was often successful and often directed his concentration towards her.

He shared this occupation with her, and she immediately felt he was the cause of her auditory hallucinations. His concentrated thought was penetrating her existence. Being outspoken, she confronted him with her fear and he merely laughed at what he considered her sense of humor. It wasn't. She only knew she had to get away from him, flee to a place of refuge where her thoughts could be guarded and only for herself.

She entered her house frantically and hurried to her dresser. She knew she could no longer live like this. She had been accumulating sleeping pills. She ingested three full bottles containing 90 pills per bottle. She lay back on the bed and drifted off. Her last thought was "finally at peace."

He never forgave himself.

Statistics

Goats cause more deaths than sharks she told herself as she entered the warm Gulf of Mexico waters. She was a good swimmer and enjoyed swimming, but this was the first time for her to enter salt water, the magical sea.

When she was offered the opportunity to transfer to Sarasota, she jumped at the chance. There was a full month to move her few belongings, and the rest of the time to spend on the beach before beginning the job as head of a children's daycare center which comprised 5 schools.

She was surprised by the amount of free time she was allowed and took full advantage of it. Despite the carefree days by the water, she researched the number of world-wide shark attacks (47) down from previous years. Then she found that in Sarasota there were two attacks in recent years. She was not discouraged by this and went seaside whenever possible.

When the month of February arrived, she and a friend decided to go to Tampa Bay for the annual Florida State Fair. She truly did not know what to expect. Upon investigating she found it possible to learn about dairy cows, pygmy goats, dairy goats, and sheep.

The goat exhibit was in progress and some of the goats were being led away to their pens. As she stepped aside for them a goat rushed toward her and butted her, knocking her unconscious.

She never recovered consciousness. All witnesses exclaimed "what a freak accident, an unusual statistic."

Inevitable

When she was a child, her father told her that the average person can unknowingly walk past 36 murderers in their lifetime. This bit of information stayed with her as she grew older. At times, she would obsess on it, never feeling fear but fascination.

In a crowd it would often cross her mind. As she made her way through a throng of people at a concert, she marveled she could have crossed paths with several murderers while there.

Pursuing a fashion career, she made the move to New York City and thought of the mass of people she would see daily. As her life in the big city was settling down into a routine, she sought entertainment for her free time. She joined a gym, took hot yoga, and took up ballroom dancing.

At times, she questioned herself why so many activities? Is it an attempt to forget that there are truly murderers out there going about their daily lives in much the same manner, as I do. And I grow older, and I realize how a fear has grown in me over time. The likelihood of an actual encounter with a killer is very slight yet there are still the words my father spoke to me those many years ago. I ask myself how many have I passed, maybe even more than 36 due to my location.

Now a forty something, her social life has been minimal. With all her activities over time she began to get to know some of the gym members and yogis. One person in yoga particularly attracted her and it appeared he was interested as well.

The friendship grew slowly, from a coffee, to walks, to dinner and a movie. They never kissed, never held hands, there was nothing particularly intimate and she found she wanted more.

Seemingly upon the spur of the moment, she invited him to her condo remarking they had never visited one another's homes. He reluctantly accepted her invitation and plans were made.

He arrived promptly and they chose a movie to stream and sat comfortably side by side occasionally commenting on an aspect of the film. When the movie ended, he suggested they watch another to which she was amenable.

As the second movie drew to a close, she became concerned when it appeared he was not preparing to leave. Remaining calm, she said, "I will show you to the door." He merely smiled and rose to follow her. When she placed her hand on the door handle, he pressed the door closed and as he looked down into her eyes, she realized she had met her murderer and vaguely wondered which number he was.

Distant Hills

She lived in a big city, doesn't matter what city, all cities were the same to her, tall buildings and a lot of people. She visited some of the mega cities, Paris, London, Madrid, Chicago and she briefly lived in New York City.

Gazing from the window, she longed with anticipation to see the bluffs of her childhood. When she left, she gave no thought to what lay before her.

Believing a megalopolis was the answer to her wanderlust, she soon realized her naiveté had led her to make a poor decision. This resolution led to disaster for her. All these thoughts flitted through her mind as she dreamed of the hills of Tennessee. Little did she know, she would never see them again.

The thought of that brought on such depression that she could not rise from her bed. She burrowed her face into the pillows and wept because there was nothing there for her now. Family was gone and no friends to tell about her desolation.

The razor cut deeply into her wrist and with each cut she felt relief and finally from loss of blood she collapsed onto the tile floor. The building superintendent found her a week later and found there was no one to contact other than the authorities. She was shuttled to the morgue and tagged, "Unclaimed Suicide."

Visitors

She worked in the dietary department of a Veteran's Hospital. It was her last year of high school. Her responsibility was to deliver the dinner trays to her patients. Some of the patients were in a large wardroom together.

It was only natural that these men would talk about the young girls delivering their food. There was one man, Brownie by name, whom she would give an extra milk occasionally. He always promised her he was going to get her a camera. A Brownie?

She came on the hospital floor one day to find that he was gone. She thought little about it and went on about her shift. She was looking forward to her next day off.

The morning started out with her Dad leaving to go to the dry cleaner, leaving her at home alone. She thought nothing of the phone ringing but was left puzzled when there was no one on the other end.

Next, within 10 minutes the doorbell rang. When she discovered it was Brownie with two other younger men, she blurted, "You can't come in, no one is home." Hearing her words, they pushed past her, entering the house.

Frantically, she watched as they entered her aunt and uncle's bedroom. They began rifling through the drawers. She knew there was a pistol in one of the places they were searching.

36

With that she heard a car door slam, and shrieked, "That is my dad, and he is going to kill all of you." Luckily, that was enough to say, and they quickly exited by the front door as her father entered through the back door. After an enthusiastic greeting, he thought it odd she was so glad to see him.

Hitchhiking

I told Michele it was a bad idea, yet she determinedly stuck out her thumb and proceeded to try to catch a ride. We were not out there on Eastern Parkway very long when an old red Volkswagen pulled up and gestured to us to get in the car.

Not wanting her to get in alone, I joined her. I took the backseat. The driver who was about our age had unruly dark hair and a beard. He said his brother was in the silver Chrysler behind us, following us.

We directed him to Michele's house, a duplex apartment in a two-story building. She and her mother and sister lived together there. We settled in the living room and were discussing music when the "brother" started wandering about the apartment. Suddenly, I heard a drawer opening in the kitchen.

My first thought was he was getting a knife. He returned to the living room, and he approached me and took my hand drawing my arm towards him. He ran the blade down my arm while asking if I wanted to die. I responded calmly that no, it would be inconvenient at this time. He said, "I don't either", and rushed down the stairs out to his car.

The friend, for I was sure they were not brothers, commented, yes, he can get weird sometimes. That was 50 years ago, and I still think about the incident and how it could have gone so very wrong.

Apricity

Being a clinomaniac, the warmth of the sun in winter was something she never knew. Particularly, on cold mornings, she had an excessive desire to stay in bed, a true clinomanic.

The year was 1600 and being a reclusive person, she only shared a few words with her family, and never with anyone, despite being introduced. She knew she had chores and would stubbornly respond to her parents with just 10 more minutes which usually turned into 30 minutes.

The father could take no more and rousted her from her bed by sunrise. Her malingering was jointly accepted by the family and as she was the youngest, they usually bowed to her wishes.

The summer would find her willing to rise as she enjoyed a warm summer day, it was the cold she loathed. That time of year was upon them and her climomania was truly powerful.

The family had all gone to the village that morning and believing her sham illness they let her remain in the cabin. They had left hurriedly and neglected to add wood to the fire upon leaving. As fate would have it, the heavy snowfall impeded their journey home. A kindly neighbor invited them in out of the cold.

They all felt assured that all was fine at home as she surely would have arisen to place wood on the fire. They became distraught when they were forced to stay the night at the neighbor's place 3 miles away.

By the time they were able to reach home, they were struck by the deadly cold of the room. They found her frozen and mourned the poor girl's death.

The Last Laugh

He had an odd sense of humor, dark humor. It could be called a cruel sense of humor. Finding delight in the misfortunes of others, he chose to say he enjoyed the irony of a bad situation.

Over time his parents believed he would learn empathy and have a kinder nature. But this was not the case, as he often chuckled about his father's old age and infirmity.

Reaching middle age did not improve his personality. His ruthless nature made him a success in his field, and he would force underlings to dine with him as a business expense.

While enjoying a sumptuous meal, he happened to notice the woman sitting at another table choking on a chicken wing. His uncontrollable laughter was so forceful that he had a heart attack followed by asphyxiation. No one mourned.

The Fall

It all began that day, when our daughter fell down the back porch stairs. She was riding her tricycle at age 5 sustaining a brain injury and days of anguish and self-reproach followed. After the danger passed, we tried to resume our busy lives.

We had done a fair amount of research on brain injuries and what to look for. We were not prepared for what we slowly began to realize about Elizabeth. She acted the same towards everyone. Strangers were not strangers to her. She could give new meaning to "she never met a stranger." It was as if she already knew them.

The mystery was finally solved concerning the girl. The doctor, who she thought was me in disguise, diagnosed her with Fregoli syndrome or Fregoli delusions. He went on to say, that Fregoli syndrome is a belief that a stranger is a familiar person. Further research revealed that the condition is named for an Italian actor Leopoldo Fregoli who was renowned for his ability to make quick changes of appearance during the stage acts.

The symptoms include visual and auditory hallucinations and problems in visual memory and motion functioning along with cognitive defects. She is prescribed an anti-psychotic and we were told that the fall she had brought about this illness.

Life continues and we know she will never have normal relationship with any stranger. We question how we will manage. Just yesterday she was leaving the yard with someone she believed was her father in disguise. Fortunately, they were stopped by me with a shout to a neighbor. Will I always be there? I can only stay vigilant.

Yulelogy

They all knew her to be a tidsoptomist, or a person that is habitually late because they think they have more time than they do. It was for that reason she was always told time an hour in advance for a rendezvous.

Well, it happened to be Christmas, and the family planned a meeting to discuss the holiday. Who is hosting, will they pitch-in or have catered, how many outsiders and finally the time. No one thought to tell her the earlier time for the meeting so naturally she missed it.

Her ears should have burned as her name was mentioned regarding her perpetual tardiness. They decided not to catch her up on matters when she finally arrived. She; therefore, never found out the time or location. When the meeting ended her question was hurriedly answered by "the usual time you should know that by now." Hearing this response, all thought it will serve her right to miss the lovely dinner we have planned to begin the evening.

Unknown to them, she told herself to arrive earlier than their usual time. So, when the gathering is at six, she schemed to surprise everyone. However, tragedy stuck, as she died from a stroke. Not a total surprise, as it was a genetic flaw.

The funeral was arranged for the third day after Christmas. The family assembled at the funeral home to bid the final goodbye to this quirky cousin. In true fashion, due to weather conditions, she arrived very late to the proceedings which all agreed was an appropriate ending.

Sonder

  She was a particularly selfish, self-serving person. She had little empathy for others and enjoyed believing her life was so much better than that of those other people. Yet, how would she know? Of her few friends, she never asked how their lives were, she just assumed that as no one confided unhappiness to her that all was fine.

  Then one day fate struck her a bizarre, and nasty blow, one which she spoke of to her friends. To her surprise, they began to open up to her as well. With that, a wave of sonder washed over her as she realized that everyone has a life as weird and complex as her own. This epiphany made her feel like she was indeed a part of the human race.

In Searching

Seeing the gravestone with the name Emma Gooch filled her with curiosity. Could that name be real or fictional as Agnes Gooch in the old movie Aunty Mame.

Her inquisitive nature drove her to research the name; she found two Emma Gooches. One held no interest for her, while the other she found fascinating. She was interested in Emma's motivations and way of going through life.

In her searching for information on Emma, she found that the grieving sister still lived and had Emmas's diary. The sister was more than willing to share the book with her as in doing so ensured that someone else took an interest in the solitary life of Emma.

While reading, she discovered that Emma had had her winter of despair. When taking up this journey, the seeker never knew that Emma had committed suicide. Within the diary was Emma's reason.

Emma was deeply curious, and she took her life in order to see what heaven looked like. Upon reading this, the woman knew that Emma would never know the answer to that question.

Petrichor

Her mind was uneasy as she drove along a particularly dangerous highway heading towards the Memorial Forest. She chose that destination for the verdure and silent beauty of the surrounding area.

Glancing at the darkening clouds, she knew that it would rain before she reached her destination. She decided it would be prudent to slow down and enjoy the raindrops as they careened down the car's windshield.

She passed billboards and was amused at the larger-than-life ads for upcoming shows at the nearby casino. She was not a gambler.

The journey proceeded as the rain continued. She thought to herself, I like the rain particularly the smell after it rains. There is a term for that she thought as she inhaled deeply. I just don't remember what it is.

Hiraeth

At an early age he knew he wanted to become an astronaut. He also knew that he would need to meet the basic requirement set by NASA. Older he set his sights on having a master's degree in a STEM field, that is science, technology, engineering or math with work experience.

He had been preparing to pass a rigorous physical examination as well. And as planned he had a strong background in pilot training. To no one's surprise, he was selected to join the space flight team. In preparation for space flight his training began with comprehensive academic studies. These studies included science, engineering and mission specific skills followed by physical conditioning and simulation training.

This all proceeded without a hitch, and with the necessary experience he now had his first important mission which was to stay at the space station orbiting the earth. He was psyched and ready to go giving little thought to the family and friends he would leave behind.

The launch and arrival were successful, and he was welcomed by the crew onboard the space station. He adapted quickly to their routine and went about his duties feeling joy at his accomplishment. But as the days wore on, he was overcome by what the Welsh call hiraeth. He became homesick for a home to which he could not return. He told himself it was a home that never really existed. He spent so much time preparing for the day and was greeted with a reality. As Thomas Wolfe said, "You can never go home again."

Foolish Wager*

It was Alexander Klivyev's manner to place bets on anything that interested him or challenged him. It rarely surprised him when he won his bets as he always believed it was a sure thing,

The morning of October 20, 1986, he bid his wife a hurried goodbye and left for the airport to meet another pilot with whom he wanted to make a wager. That was all life was to him; you were lucky or you weren't and he considered himself among the lucky.

He knew Kurumoch Airport well and decided he would put money on the bet that he could land using an instrument only approach. First officer Zhimov was doubtful and hesitantly accepted the wager thinking there is no way that Alexander would attempt such a thing as there was too much at stake.

He realized the approach was being made with the cockpit windows closed so there was no view of the ground as they attempted to land. In fright, he listened to air traffic control's advice warning to abort the landing but to no avail. The plane flipped over and caught fire, killing 70 of the 94 people on board.

Naturally, the incident was investigated, and it was determined that Klivyev's arrogance contributed to the loss of lives. He received a 15-year prison sentence shortened to 6 years. One would hope he never flew again.

*This is based on information recently disclosed by the KGB.

Plaster Saints

She was given the "In Loving Memory" card as she entered the memorial service for Owen Thomas. There were many in attendance, and some familiar faces turned acknowledging her while others viewed her with interest or curiosity.

As the minister spoke about Owen's life portraying him as a loving son, husband, father and grandfather there were sighs of remembrance. No one could deny the man's goodness.

She alone knew of his conflicting feelings toward the congregation. He spoke to her about it confidentially. Why he chose to disclose those admissions to her she did not know but he did explain saying "I know you are a good listener."

Her lack of judgement involving him was not so difficult to comprehend. She had been at the mercy of many of the church members as they judged, gossiped, and spoke of her in demeaning terms. She realized these people did not know her in any sense of the word. She was unmarried and childless, which caused many to raise an eyebrow. She never felt she needed to give an explanation. Her credo was "live and let live." She felt there were many who thought that way as well.

As a pillar of society, Owen heard many life stories. He never pried and never questioned why she did not tell him her story; he accepted her reticence to speak about herself.

To everyone's surprise, Owen had written a letter to be read to those attending the funeral. The beginning sentence drew much attention as people's names were loudly read. Some blushed, others hung their heads while others grinned foolishly. None expected what followed.

They were all told in no uncertain terms that they were a disappointment to society. They were an assorted collection of hypocrites. The minister continued with contempt ignoring that his name was among the many referenced. His hypocrisy knows no bounds.

In closing the letter read, "May you all burn in hell." This left no question as to the letter's sincerity. To complete the picture, she was the only one who laughed and cried simultaneously. There was only silence from the others.

"It's Too Late Now"

She heard that said by a woman speaking to her child. She wondered how often that phrase had been cast at someone. It can be said vindictively or ironically. It works well as a retort.

Sadly, it is so often true, and matters are beyond repair. Words cannot be retracted as the damage is done. A reminder from the one to whom the deed has been confided.

Do we look back? Do we consider alternatives to a decision made or is it truly too late now?

The extent to which this aphorism can be stated can vary. Too late to brew a pot of tea or too late to tell someone you love them. We are so often reminded to seize the day and at the end of the day, curled up in your bed. do you think "it is too late now?"

The Wayward Christian

He defined himself as a wayward Christian, explaining that he was raised in a Christian household, yet never really found peace or comfort in pursuing the religion. At the age of 12 he stopped attending Sunday school as his parents decided it was his decision.

In later years, at the age of 30, he decided to read a book that had been given to his father many years previously. It was a book by Lloyd Douglas entitled The Robe. Within the pages of this book, he found that what he was always missing, faith.

As he read that Christ turned the water into wine, he realized that the water had not been changed to wine it was the people's faith that caused them to be believe in the phenomenon.

He neither confronted nor ridiculed those faithful to their religion. He just accepted that he would rather view Christianity as the path to saving the soul. He felt if he caused no one harm, that at the end he would find peace albeit not salvation.

He passed through life with few regrets feeling at the end of life he would finally rest in peace. He did think of his final days, often, believing upon the last breath any mystery would be solved. It pleased him to think that at the end there would be nothing. He would not have a tormented soul and was convinced of this. What frustrated him was that he knew that he would not be able to contact anyone to let them know there is nothing after all.

Much to his friend's surprise as they stood at this bedside, in his final moments he cried out, "Christ forgive me," then winked and confided, "just in case."

Tragic End

They had been friends since elementary school and occasionally chatted on the phone. As the school years passed, she grew increasing heavy and he became increasingly shy.

Junior high school went uneventfully for the most part. She noticed he accelerated academically while she became the butt of school jokes. He found that she did not attend school very often.

By high school her school attendance was brought to the attention of her concerned parents. His parents were concerned for him but for entirely different reasons. He felt isolated and alone. Both felt persecuted, as well as, ridiculed.

Darren's father was a successful doctor, and the boy found the bottle of sleeping pills in his medical case. He swallowed the entire bottle and closed himself in his locker to die. His body was discovered two days later.

She would never discuss his death.

Comes in Three

April, May, and June were triplets born approximately 10 minutes apart. Each baby had its own unique cry, laugh and smile. As they were identical triplets this was the only manner by which to tell them apart.

April distinguished herself with a shrieking lament, a snorting laugh, and a crooked smile, while May wept profusely, laughed quietly and had more of a grimace than a smile. On the other hand, June howled when laughing and as she cried, tears fell gently down her cheeks, her smile was a broad grin. These differences were noticeable to all who encountered them whether in school or on the playground. It was a remarkable contrast among the three.

As they grew older, their once shared interests began to change, in simple aspects and more complex as well. While April disliked watching television, May wouldn't miss her favorite shows and June only liked going to the cinema.

April found swarthy, tall boys attractive, and May liked blonde hair and fair-skin boys, June didn't like boys at all. The examples of their opposite tastes could be lengthy, so just say, by 18 they each had changed but only in opinions.

April loved to travel and had plans to get a Eurorail Pass and see Europe over the entire summer. May sought and found a summer job working as a lifeguard at a local pool. June preferred playing on a softball team and bike riding at the summer camp she attended. So the girls bid one another a fond goodbye and sincere wishes they would all have a splendid summer.

Odd to think that were separated by location only to be reunited at death. As April raced across a busy Parisian street, she was struck and killed by a speeding motorist. In trying to save a young boy whose head had disappeared beneath the water, May was accidentally drowned. June met her last when struck in the head by a ball which was not so soft. Oddly each girl in corresponding time zones died at 11:11. Viewed in their caskets, to everyone's dismay, no one could tell them apart.

Dinnertime

Donald regularly made his visits about the time we sat down to dinner. This was generally a Thursday night. He would enter through the back door onto the porch then appear on the door sill to the kitchen.

There he was, frozen T.V. dinner in-hand looking pitiful. Naturally, we told him to join us, and he readily accepted the invitation. Much to our amusement, we found we were not the only ones to receive these dinnertime visits.

Trying to empathize I decided Donald disliked eating alone and preferred sharing our dinner rather than the frozen meal he carried to our house. We noted it was always the same, roast beef, mashed potatoes, gravy and peas and carrots.

One Thursday when he arrived, I was in no mood for niceties and took his dinner, microwaved it and told him to enjoy it as we did not have enough. He did so obediently. I think back on this sadly as several years later we lost Donald and miss him to this day.

The Brothers

The fifth of bourbon was clenched in the fist of one of them. Both thought it would make it easier to take spending any amount of time together. They each filled a shot glass and threw their heads back as they gulped the powerful liquid.

Their eyes met as they lowered their glasses. Each tried a smile but knew it was hopeless. So, the oldest opened the conversation with Dad preferred you, talked to you and took you fishing while he left me at home with Mother.

The younger of the two retorted yes well Mother favored you. She probably persuaded Dad to leave you with her. That idea had never occurred to the elder boy.

They each took another shot, liking it as the warmth spread through their limbs. Feeling the necessity for sincerity, they admitted in turn that despite differences they had genuinely cared for one another. This time the smile spread their features and was heartfelt.

Odd that each of them had considered punching the other and never seeing each other again, now all was different, and a calmness filled the room. At last, a happy ending.

Love

We spoke on the phone for a long time. It had been years, so we had a lot to catch up on. He told me his next birthday he would be 89. I stated my age too, he responded, "I know," sounding amazed at the passage of time.

Drew and I worked together in a recording studio for the blind. He was a narrator and worked at one of the local radio stations as well. He is now a retired news reporter.

Drew did not originally pursue a career in radio. He was a Catholic priest and had his seminary days at St Meinrad in Southern Indiana. I knew this and in conversation with him I asked where he lived, he said "Tell City." I honestly thought he meant Rome, Italy as a symbol of his devotion to the church and confession.

In the early years of his priesthood, he met a young woman and was smitten. He left the priesthood, not the church, and they were married. Now three grown children later, he feels he has so much to be grateful for.

As we chatted, he remarked, that during the years of the pandemic, it was just Drew and his wife Mary alone together in their home. He lowered his voice and said timidly, "We are so in love." My response, "That is beautiful."

Phobias

She wondered if she had a phobia about phobias. Upon researching it, nothing was found so it was safe to assume it did not exist. While researching the topic she found many fascinating phobias which brought to mind fears of others also including herself.

Discovering that there are over 500 phobias, she decided to limit her search to those listed as rare. Upon asking the 5 most common phobias, she was told there is arachnophobia (fear of spiders). She knows several that exhibit this fear. Next is ophidiphobia (the fear of snakes) which she knew firsthand about suffering from that, as do so many others. Glossophobia (the fear of public speaking) was another phobia she felt others share and also found it is the most common. Naturally, acrophobia (the fear of heights) was among the list.

She however, did not have that fear. Finally, there is social phobia (the fear of social interactions) too many to name with that malady. She did know about gatophobia (the fear of cats) as she had witnessed this reaction from others to her own cat.

It came as no surprise when reading that a phobia is a type of anxiety disorder. It can be caused by a past incidence or trauma; it can also be a learned response from early life. It is a reaction to fear and the result of long-term stress. There are even genetic factors.

Finding her obsession with phobias disturbing she decides to discuss this with a therapist; she makes an appointment with someone recommended to her by her general practitioner. Relief was felt when a woman was recommended.

The appointment was for the following week and her anxiety increased as she anticipated the meeting. Fretting about what to share and more important what not to share, she paced the floor.

When the day arrived, she thought there would be a feeling of relief rather than the dread she felt. It was enough to prevent her from going. She was afraid of what she might learn about herself. The therapist waited 20 minutes then knew it was not going to happen. It was not the first time for someone to be a no-show. There was pity on the therapist's face as she crossed the name off her books thinking, there is nothing to fear but fear itself.

Elementary

The balding, bespectacled man led the prospective patient into his consulting room; the year was 1900. This visitor was familiar with the doctor's work in the field of psychology. He had looked forward to seeing the father of psychoanalysis. As a matter of fact, the recently published Interpretation of Dreams was the reason the tall, slender man had made an appointment.

After being ushered into the room, he withdrew his clay pipe from his pocket and placed it in this mouth, preparing to ignite the fragrant tobacco. The doctor did not object, so he carried on.

The caller, dressed in a tweed suit, ulster, deerstalker hat and Inverness cape spoke in a rush of words. His piercing eyes and thin hawk-like nose presented an imposing figure. Speaking in his high-pitched voice he said he was there to discuss a recurring dream. He continued with "I have read your book on interpreting dreams and wish to undergo psychoanalysis."

The doctor listened patiently asking no questions. He merely nodded and encouraged the speaker to continue if the story was halted when the patient searched for a word or became lost in thought.

The dream is rather dramatically disclosed. The case involved the disturbing dream that Sherlock had been having about Dr. Watson, his longtime partner and confidant. Watson insists that Sherlock Holmes does not exist. His life depends on the pen of a Sir Arthur Conan Doyle. As the story ended, he merely begged for the doctor to make something of his dream.

Finally, his plea was answered by Dr. Freud. As Holmes is told, your dream is intuitive and indeed you do not exist. Only in the mind of readers. Your methods and mannerisms are based upon a Dr. James Best, a professor at the medical school Doyle attended. Just as you are depicted, this master of diagnostics was known to make broad conclusions from minute observations.

Fraught with anxiety and not believing the doctor's words, he rushed from the room and vanished.

Opinionated

He was an ultracrepidarian while she was sapiosexual. He had opinions on matters that he knew nothing about. She, in her naive fashion, sought to share his opinions never dreaming that they were totally inaccurate. So, her attraction to intelligence was also misguided.

It was truly sad to hear the fellow expound his opinions on climate change, denying it's existential threat. There is also his belief that education is not an equalizer, and he denied the right to freedom of speech.

He believed that the earth is going through a warming period, and it is nothing to worry about as he scoffs at protestors. This ties in with his believing that education is reserved for those that can afford it. He belittles scholarships and seeking a higher education for those who had little wealth.

These opinions confirmed that he believed that only a better education should be available to the affluent and those that have the right to speak out exercising the freedom of speech should have deep pockets.

Finally, she woke up to the reality that he had many opinions and those were wrong. She grimaces when he inhales to begin his diatribe on unsubstantiated ideologies. She went on a quest for critical thinking, leaving him, still talking, far behind.

The Act of Suicide

He didn't know what to make of it. He loved her but her constant unsuccessful suicide attempts left him inconsolable. When he questioned her, "Why?". she merely shrugged her shoulders and replied, "It is something to do." Next followed his query "Am I not enough to give you a feeling of fulfillment? This longing for death mystifies me." These remarks always left her wanting to succeed in taking her life. She was left with questioning herself and her motives. Do I do it for the attention? she questions.

Her conclusion was eventually the necessity to succeed never thinking of the consequences of such an act, until her sister stated, "Do you know how devastating this would be for all the people that love you?" Ironically, he was the last person she thought of when told this.

Disliking the idea of a painful suicide, she had been saving sleeping pills for a successful suicide...her final attempt. The cut wrists and then leaving the car running for carbon monoxide poisoning along with running out in traffic to the sound of screeching tires did nothing but frustrate her. She considered herself a chicken, but the sleeping pills it must be.

He finally came to the decision to help and even accompany her. When he proposed this to her, she was so repulsed that she became determined to live and not torture him and her family with impending doom. They lived their lives out happily and when their time did come, they died within an hour of one another.

The Plea

"Don't leave me" she begged as he walked out the door suitcase in hand. There was no other woman, nothing sordid as that. He just wanted a different life, one that did not involve attachment. This thinking; however, brought discontent for both of them. He found no joy in living independently, but he was too proud to admit it to her,

The time they spent apart grew longer and each began to realize this separation was what each of them needed. He followed his desire to write while she took painting classes and was pleased with the artwork she produced.

Time passed quickly and to their surprise 5 years had passed. Divorce was out of the question as both took their wedding vows seriously enough not to end their bond. When he knew that it was the perfect moment to suggest a reconciliation, she remembered her plea not to leave her.

After a brief text, she asked him to come for a tea in order to determine what would come next. He knew he was going to ask for reconciliation. While she had come to her own decision about the planned meeting.

He embraced her warmly when she opened the door upon his arrival. She asked him to seat himself in the kitchen, where they often met in the past, for a serious discussion.
She poured the tea and offered a plate of pastries. As they drank the tea, he became flushed and told her he felt unwell. He

then collapsed with head and arms on the table in front of him. Her final thought after drinking the poisoned tea was "Now you will never leave me again."

In Dreams

It was an exhausting day, an argument with her partner, a dressing down at work and now she is late getting home to prepare dinner. On the way home, she catches every stoplight as she thinks over the entire day finding it frustrating and sad.

The evening meal was shared in mutual contempt and silence. In order to avoid conversation, she turned on a movie for them both to watch. The plot, the dialogue, all escaped her as she obsessed thinking of the disagreement they had had earlier. A trivial misunderstanding she told herself, really amounts to nothing. She decided against mentioning the matter and the evening passed uneventfully.

Time for bed, she told herself, you deserve a good night's sleep. The partner was going out to run a few forgotten errands and left.

Lying down, she began to relax and experienced hypnogogic imaging which occurs in the transitional state from wakefulness to sleep. This can also be called the waning state of consciousness during the onset of sleep.

These individual images are often fleeting, and it was during this shift from wakefulness that she briefly saw her partner being confronted by someone unknown to her. That was all and she drifted off to sleep. Hours later she was awakened by the ring of her phone. She reached for it and heard the person telling her that her partner had been robbed at gunpoint and was shot and killed while resisting.

She immediately thought of the image she experienced and realized it was a premonition. She thought another dream which means nothing. She rolled over and went back to sleep. Impossible, she thought on awakening and jarringly realized he was not in bed beside her.

She chastised herself as she returned the call she had received earlier and was told she needed to come to the morgue to identify her partner. In shock, she agreed to do so.

After seeing his lifeless body and feeling reassured as she gazed at his relaxed features, she believed he felt neither fear nor pain. She drove slowly home.

The rest of the day passed in a blur again she felt such guilt and accepted she was in denial about the late night phone call. Besides she told herself there was nothing she could have done, yet the dream continued to haunt her.

As evening drew near, she was anxious to get to sleep, to close out the events of the past few days. From their argument Io his violent death, she blamed herself for insensitivity. After hours of tossing and turning, she finally went to sleep. Again, she had the hypnogogic imaging seeing herself struck by a car.

In the past she was prone to somnambulism and this night due to the stress, she rose from her bed around 2 a.m. and began sleepwalking. She walked out of the house, crossing the street only to be plowed down by a speeding car. This ended her life and her disturbing premonitions.

The Nemophilist

It was a fluffle of rabbits and a charm of finches that greeted her as she entered the forest. Her eyes were bright with anticipation.

The sanitarium sat next to this lovely, wooded area and she ventured to go away from the hospital grounds. She wanted to disappear; to no longer participate in the life she was living. There were moments of clarity for her, and she realized she was incarcerated for erratic behavior.

She knows the symptoms and is able to describe them. Simple really, she explains. My insomnia increases and the prescribed pills do not work. She is cautioned never to take more than one. Next, loss of appetite, nothing stimulates hunger and finally the thought of food makes her stomach turn. And then this is followed by hallucinations. She is unable to decipher the real from the unreal. This time, she was able to tell a family member, she was considering suicide and agreed to be committed.

The ward's medications made her zombie-like so she quit taking her medicine by deftly hiding the pills in her hand and quickly transferring them to a pocket to later be emptied into the toilet. She had not taken any medication for a month.

As she walked slowly along, her forest loving personality sought refuge in the woods as she heard nurses and aides calling for her. She ran to a tree and quickly scaled it, ignoring the painful scratches from the branches. She climbed ever higher until looking below she was convinced no one would find her. As she balanced there the branch suddenly gave way and she fell to the ground striking her head on the boulder below. The sound drew the searchers attention, and they rushed to her side. Surprisingly she was conscious and uttered in her last breath "I am glad it is ending this way."

Inciting the End

She felt like the Alaskan Wood frog that freezes in winter and thaws, to live again, in spring. That was the effect spring had on her, and she believed that many people underwent that same renaissance.

Each day she saw changes in the outdoor planters. The lilies were emerging from the ceramic pots on the front porch. Spring and the green plants begin to bloom. The array of daffodils greets her in the morning walks around the garden. Plans were made about what to dig up and move and what to feed nutrients.
'
No plans are made to travel during this season. She wants to plant, cultivate and enjoy her passion for gardening.

Spring moves colorfully into summer and the garden has passed into another phase. The yellow iris are in bloom as are the purple iris, and soon the azalea and anemones will announce their presence.

Feeling nearly overwhelming love for the garden, she begins thinking about sitting solitary and enjoying the evening breeze. The days grow warmer, and the night sky was beautiful on a clear night.

All wondered why she chose to sit in the garden that night, when her sister had warned her there was a rapist in the area and to lock her doors carefully,

She felt no fear when she heard the garden gate open. A tall man, just as her sister described, rushed to her sitting calmly in her lawn chair. It was then she shot him right between the eyes.

You Just Never Know

Staring at him intently for some time, she realized he had dark eyes like Rilke. She did not dare approach him, but hoped someone would engage him in conversation so that she could listen in.

She was becoming obsessed with wanting to know his interests, his likes and dislikes. At times she found this exhilarating and at other times, depressing,

If she let herself fall in love with him, she knew she could not bear it. Her heart had never been broken, and this was no time to experience that now.

Then it happened, he was not immune to her furtive glances and her blush whenever their eyes met. He asked her out. As he was relatively new in town, he asked her choice of somewhere to go for dinner. They chose a restaurant near the park where they could walk after their meal.

Dining pleasantly in a candlelit room, he joked with her sotto voce about the others enjoying the ambiance. She thought it odd and cruel, but she also thought we are just at the getting to know one another stage.

He remained polite with her and held the door for her as they exited. She was relieved that he did not try to take her hand. as they strolled the paths. She began to relax.

Suddenly he stopped walking and placed his hands on her shoulders, turning her to face him. It was then he wrapped his fingers around her throat strangling the life out of her. He lay her gently on the ground and walked away.

Headache?

When researching the Tylenol Murders, I found that the case was never solved. I also found that 7 Chicago-area residents died after swallowing capsules laced with potassium cyanide. The year was 1982. Odd that three of the victims had the first name of Mary. Obviously, the perpetrator had no control over this.

The suspect, James Lewis, was arrested in 1982 but denied any involvement. However, he did send a letter to the manufactures of Tylenol demanding $1 million to, "Stop the killing."

The suspect, Lewis, was never charged with the murders; but he did serve more than 12 years in prison for the extortion note he sent to Johnson and Johnson.

Fortunately, no copycat killings have occurred since that fateful day.
Or have they?

The Freezer

The day it was delivered was a special day for Beatrice. She had wanted a 300 lb. freezer for several years and finally made the decision to purchase one to have in the basement. Her husband Burt, complained as usual, despite her argument supporting the acquisition. He refused to be there when the appliance was delivered. Feeling pleased with herself, Beatrice went shopping in order to purchase various meats to place in the new freezer. When Burt returned home in his sulking mood, he decided he would make Beatrice's life miserable, or even more so.

The cruelty went on for months and he never admitted the advantages of having the freezer. Slowly, a plan began to form in Beatrice's mind. She wanted to be rid of this constantly nagging husband.

Burt considered himself quite the handyman, so after removing most of the frozen items from the freezer, she persuaded him to climb up on a step ladder and enter the freezer in order to remove a few frozen vegetables that she claimed were frozen solid to the bottom. Gloating that his help was needed and that at long last she had to admit it was a mistake to purchase this addition to their home he did as she wished,

Burt was able to climb into the freezer and as he was upon his hands and knees he began to pry the frozen food from the freezer bottom. It was then she plunged the freshly sharpened knife into his back. He collapsed and she quickly shut the freezer door on him.

Beatrice's effort to stab Burt did not end his life, and he began to scream and beat on the freezer top demanding release as she piled bricks upon this instrument of death. Finally, his voice weakened. Perhaps he was resigned to the fact that he was going to die in the much hated freezer. Beatrice patiently waited several days just to be certain her plan worked and Burt was indeed dead. Now was the second part of her plan.

She slowly removed the bricks and cautiously opened the lid of the freezer. Much to her satisfaction, Burt was dead with a look of rage upon his face. She then replaced the once frozen food stuffs upon his lifeless body, waited an additional several days to call the junkman to haul away the freezer which she claimed had never worked properly.

No sooner than the truck pulled away, she grabbed her already packed valise and headed to the airport. She left the car in the long-term parking lot that she knew she would never return to get.

Her flight to Finland was just the next stop in her plan. During the flight she was questioned why Finland? She replied, "I have always loved the cold."

Memento Mori

"Don't ever laugh as a hearse goes by, for you may be the next to die"-memorable lyrics to The Hearse Song. How much time do I have left on this planet, Sadie asked herself while humming the melody to this song.

Morbid thoughts for one so young, but inevitable as she has encountered many deaths already in her young life. There was the boy that committed suicide at the high school they attended. He left no note just closed himself in one of the lockers after taking a large amount of sleeping pills.

Another boy she had known since childhood was thrown from a speeding car and killed. He was 16. She watched her uncle holding the hand of her great-grandmother who was dying. When she was told she would see the departed relative again, she replied "No I won't." The time came when she no longer had any living relatives.

The inevitability of death drew her thoughts unexpectedly. She never spoke to anyone about it, but felt justified in pretending that life is meant to be enjoyed. Her only enjoyment came from imagining her final hour and drawing her last breath.

She never asked herself if she needed help, needed counseling. Her fate was and would always be in her hands. It was the one matter in which she felt in total control. Her plan was simple because she had a prescription for sleeping pills. Once she had accumulated enough, she would take an overdose. The time came she did and was found dead two days later.

No one was surprised. The note she left only said, "I wanted to call the shots on this one—goodbye."

A Madness Malady

Naturally, it does not go unnoticed that "lady" makes up most of the word malady. And yes, from Bertha, the madwoman in the attic to Lorena Bobbit's temporary insanity plea, it is quite well-known not to anger a woman.

Mike was one husband that would learn that lesson, she thought as she planned to be acquitted with a temporary insanity plea after killing him. Ironically, Mike had the same idea ending with an insanity appeal as well.

Both had been setting the scene for friends to observe their newfound devotion to one another. It would be convincing enough for an insanity plea to be justified in the eyes of the law.

Relatives questioned one another as to, "What is going on?" The critical complaints they heard so often were replaced by false praise. Of course, the two were so busy complimenting each other that neither considered the truth in these actions.

Each had a pistol that often came to mind as they gazed at each other. But that was as far as their plans took them. At times the desire to get the gun, aim it, and pull the trigger was overwhelming for both of them.

After a few months of false affection, the ruse began to wear on them. Their tones grated on the nerves of this faux man and wife experiencing marital bliss. Then when alcohol came into play no one could predict the outcome.

It was amazing that the two thought so much alike as each brought home a bottle of bourbon thinking this would ease the tension of being together. They had no intention of offering the other a drink but chose to have several big gulps before encountering the other.

Fueled by the liquor each called to the other out to the living room, pistols drawn. Time for a show down. There was no time for a show down as each fired simultaneously killing their partner. The killings were ruled by reason of insanity.

Quest

Do people sometimes, out of sheer boredom, long for something to happen to shake up their world a bit? Caution, that is the trail of dangerous thinking. The following is just such a tale.

Laura yearned for just such an experience to enliven her mere existence on earth. She decided to take up hitchhiking. She thought the adventure would be worth the risk. She would meet new people as well as travel without cost. Her decision to hitch a ride from Washington to Oregon seemed the perfect plan.

Standing by the highway, she stuck out her thumb and within a short time a 1968 Volkswagen Beetle pulled over to allow her admittance to the car. She did not hesitate and jumped in the car quickly as she saw the driver was a nice-looking, dark-haired man with a kind smile. She knew no sense of dread as he introduced himself as Ted.

Lexicon

Do people still say ,"How could you?", or "You wouldn't dare?"

Simply put, do we still resort to 1940's film noir dialogue? Is this a cynics point of view? May I ask you to tea, in order to discuss archaic terms in today's world?

"Well, I never!" This retort may have happily ended many a conversation, but today, not so much. Could it be because fewer people can say they have never committed some unnamable sin?

And by sin, are you referring to the Seven deadly Sins? They certainly tell a tale of woe. Don't look inside yourself too long. Are we not human, do we not survive to thrive to test limits?

I rant and I can't deny it but inspired by a lively conversation and exchanging ideas with others.

The Secret

"Elisabeth," he called to his wife as she hurried down the steps to avoid any confrontation. In her hurry, she fell forward on the last few steps. More embarrassed than hurt, she rushed on. He continued calling out to her but to no avail.

What had he said for her to react to his seemingly harmless words. It was not what he said, it was what he didn't say. There were many things he didn't say such as "You look pretty today," or "Is that a new dress? It looks nice." In truth it wasn't a slight, he just never noticed. On the other hand, she was very demonstrative in their relationship.

She grew cold towards him, which caused scenes and accusations., Issues were never resolved. When he said something she did not want to hear, she turned her head away. He found it annoying. Confronting her, all she could do was run from him. She wanted to escape this moment of truth. She had to tell him there was someone else.

She neglected to see the oncoming car and was hit and would die a few hours later, never saying a word. He mourned her and never knew her secret.

Souls

As the soul is regarded as immortal because it is the spiritual or immaterial part of a human being, we may believe that death is just one step in a soul's journey through the universe.

So, when these two souls met, they both realized this was no ordinary meeting. Their eyes met, their breath caught, and they both swallowed sharply.

Lizzie Owens is an amusing woman. She is outspoken and does not suffer fools gladly. Ralph Croft was not so amusing as he was interesting. He pursues his interest thereby, making him a fascinating character. To them it was a day, just a day, so there was nothing unusual about the meeting.

Then, as can happen, they were introduced to one another by a mutual friend. The friend thought nothing about the introduction or what the result would be; it was common courtesy to introduce them when the two were drawn into conversation.

It was a party of sorts or more like a meeting of people considered either amusing or interesting. And after the introduction and conversing, Ralph found Lizzie amusing and Lizzie found Ralph interesting.

It was Lizzie's smile that Ralph found whimsical; and her gentle laugh beguiling, in addition he found her wish to save the world one person at a time entertaining. On the other hand, Lizzie became captivated by Ralph because of his interest in Arctic travels. He wanted to put together an expedition to photograph wildlife.

As the evening wore on, they realized they had been talking to one another exclusively for quite some time. Each agreed to leave the party as it was getting late.

Ralph saw Lizzie to her car, and they decide to have coffee soon. Yet they never met again. Something intuitively told each of them that it would mean only heartbreak ahead.

Friends that knew the two of them wondered why nothing had come of the burgeoning relationship between Lizzie and Ralph. Ralph went on to try to discover himself while photographing polar bears of the Arctic while Lizzie became a case worker in domestic disputes. The details of their simultaneous deaths mystified their acquaintances, as at the same moment Ralph was mauled and killed by a polar bear, Lizzie was brutally murdered by an irate couple she was attempting to counsel. The two souls, alike in character and temperament, were never meant to share their lives together thought the friends as they shook their heads.

It's a Sign

The friends were sharing a meal and sharing ideas. One of them liked to write and would often share the words she had committed on paper with her friend., The conversation resulted in the one friend encouraging the other with you could write anything, you could write about that sign.

Feeling her imagination challenged, she decided to indeed write a story not so much about the sign but the fellow that made the sign—the sign maker as it were.

Upon researching the topic, she found sign makers create designs, lettering and graphics using software program machines to cut, shape and mould materials.

Well, this certain sign maker, Bill Matthews, was a master craftsman and had completed his apprenticeship in Signage. He also studied painting and decorating in order to gain sign writing skills.

He sought and found work with a local sign company in his hometown. At the age of 25 he was gainfully employed and had a weekly income. After working with signs such as billboards and painting designs on the side of buildings, he was confident in his work and enjoyed it.

The assignment that day was to paint a sign on the side of a building. He and another worker put up the scaffolding while inspecting the building's wall for anything that would impede their progress.

The work began near the roof of the building and was extremely high, but Bill paid no attention; he felt no fear. He was speaking animatedly to the other worker about the previous night's basketball game. As he demonstrated the winning shot, he accidentally stepped off the scaffold and plunged to his death when he landed his neck broke.

The service for him was brief and everyone agreed, he was a good sign maker, the salt of the earth. He was mourned by a wife and child who did not know the job was dangerous.

Mania

He was a loner preferring his own company to that of others. His days passed and the mania continued. He had not known the depths of depression for quite some time.

His spirits always lifted when he entered the cemetery. He considered it his neighborhood. It was his comfort zone. As he had partial hearing loss, he didn't wear headphones but walked along with his phone playing Pandora radio. If he approached others walking in the cemetery, he silenced the streaming radio program.

It was explained to him that his bouts of depression were so deep that he hallucinated; he created his own world. It was a world of distrust and terror for him as he viewed everyone he encountered as having hateful feelings towards him; he felt threatened and retreated even more. It is unknown why his sudden manic phrase was quickly followed by depression.

As he walked the cemetery paths, he felt he was finally alone there as he saw no one else. He approached a group of people he suddenly spied. They ignored him, which convinced him that he was invisible. The people were gathered around the grave of a well-known personality, and they had left their SUV running as they did not plan to be there long.

Discovering what he considered an abandoned car, he hopped in and drove hastily through the narrow paths of the cemetery. He was not accustomed to driving much less such a large vehicle and at high speed and had a head on collision with a solid oak tree. The car crumpled, trapping him beneath the tree. He breathed his last as security tried to free him from the wreckage. The evening news covered this tragedy, yet no one attended his funeral except his psychiatrist.

Ear Worm

It was unsettling for Elaine that whenever she saw her neighbor she hears sinister music reverberate in her ears. She did not understand why she had these misgivings toward her neighbor as they had only exchanged words a few times. Is it intuition that causes one to distrust another person that they barely know?

There were signs, all the different cars in the driveway. The men that stayed long into the night. She became obsessed with watching what was happening next door.

One night she returned home to discover an unknown car parked in her driveway. Not wishing to block the car she parked in the easement beneath the crab-apple tree.

She grew concerned that the license plate read temporary and there were printed signs in the car window saying that the driver had his driver's license. Feeling this might have something to do with the neighbor, she telephoned the police. They arrived, checked out the vehicle, and called for a tow-truck.

She was glad the car was gone from her driveway, but shortly thereafter was apprehensive when there came a knock on her door. The man standing there demanded to know where his car was and became non-plussed with the news that the police had towed the car away. When the neighbor joined them on the front porch, the music sounded again in her ears. The two headed back towards her house; she was apparently a friend of this guy.

They were in her front yard when their shouts could be heard. The woman's shrill shrieks ended with the sound of a gun being fired, he collapsed, and the neighbor stood over him laughing. She placed her foot on his chest and raised her hands in the air exclaiming, "It was self-defense," which any witness would refute. It was hate that pulled that trigger and it was the conclusion the woman came to—her neighbor was truly sinister after all.

The Recyclers

At one time recyclables were collected in small orange containers. It was during this time that he was a sanitation worker and found that he could gain information about the recycler just by paying attention to the items discarded for recycling.

Some people will meticulously place articles in the bin and others pay scant attention. He noticed this and formed opinions. When he was assigned to a different neighborhood, he looked forward to the possibility of discovering new things that had been tossed out.

This first day brought a surprising development. One of the bins had an empty wine bottle, a wine he bought routinely. He saw that the seltzer water was the same he brought home from the grocery. Then there was the milk carton, his brand. He stared in amazement as he discovered each object was a product he bought regularly. He was determined to meet the person that had his exact tastes.

After work he found himself ringing the doorbell of the recycler. He was pleasantly surprised when the door was opened by an attractive woman that looked at him questioningly.

He proceeded to explain why he was there and expressed his interest in her as they apparently had identical likes. He wondered about dislikes. She listened patiently to his explanation then asked if he would like to join her for a cup of Earl Grey. Naturally, that was a favorite tea for them both.

This was the beginning of a compatible relationship. They spent the rest of their lives together.

The Disappearance

Her vacant look, her distant voice, her nervous laughter, and indulgent smile, all defined her to the attentive observer. Paul was an attentive observer and found her fascinating. Little did he know she prayed to die and longed for a different atmosphere. One filled with the gaiety that seemed to escape her.

Paul set out to know her better by inviting her for a coffee. He planned to ask her why she never attended the parties given by mutual friends. He prefaced the invitation with a claim that he wanted her opinion on the state of the world. He admitted it seems like a weak approach but could think of nothing else to say.

Initially, she was reluctant to accept his invitation, but in this case perseverance had its reward, and she agreed to a morning coffee. They would meet at the coffee shop; she felt this safer for her and told him she would walk there for the rendezvous.

Paul was unsure of himself, a feeling he rarely knew. He was unsure what to say to her or how to draw her out. He decided to try to get her to talk about herself, her interests and plans for the future. For the most part, she kept her responses to monosyllables, and when she said she had no plans for the future, he grew impatient.

After she agreed to take a drive with him, her mood seemed to change. She even asked if they could ride out and see the old, wooden bridge. He forgot his impatience with her and turned in the direction of the bridge.

Once the bridge was in sight, she became excited and asked if they could walk out on it. Again he acquiesced, but decided not to join her. When they got there, she quickly exited the car approaching the bridge determinedly. He watched her from the car, waving her onward.

She suddenly turned and looking at him dispassionately simply disappeared. When the shock wore off, he ran to the place on the bridge where she was standing. He peered over the side into the rushing water of the river and saw nothing but white water. She was gone.

Slowly, he returned to the car and drove back to town. His explanation for her vanishing was not believed and he was arrested in connection with her disappearance. He spent the rest of his life behind bars.

Those that visit the bridge, claim to hear her nervous laughter. Some even believe she was the ghost of a woman that jumped from the bridge many years in the past. No one has ever questioned Paul's guilt but there are those that claim his innocence.

Just Chatting

She stared at the brightly colored tablecloth as she arranged the bowl of sliced apples before him. He rarely visited and wondering what it was about caused the slight ripple in her forehead that he knew well.

A frequent wish when in his presence, she hoped for a conversation in which neither of them had to work. Smiling, she said, "Why don't we just exchange pleasantries?" One could say he was shocked into submission and complied.

Their conversation included discussing the flowers in bloom and the progress of the garden. It did not take long for the talk to dwindle and they were left facing one another. The silence persisted and they shared a nervous smile. Reluctantly, he asked if they should begin a heart-to-heart and she agreed.

Then came forth a rush of words from him declaring his love for her. She turned her head away from him not wishing to hear anymore.

It infuriated him and he grabbed one of the fist-sized rocks nearby and brought it down on her head, smashing her skull. Then he slowly walked away leaving her on the deck. He was telling himself no one would connect him to her death; he got in his car and drove away. Besides. he rationalized; we were just chatting.

A Situation

He was a sadistic sort, one that sought and found work where he could inflict pain and hurt others. He sought jobs bringing him into contact with people in need of help. His jobs consisted of an orderly in a hospital, a lab tech that drew blood, an assembly line worker in a factory and a physical therapist. He loved the irony of working in the health care industry.

He moved from town to town and hospital to hospital when complaints about him begin to mount. He worked the longest at a factory as no one could trace who was making the tops of the aspirin bottles impossible to open.

This started when he was 25; before that, he only dreamed of harming others including his parents and schoolmates. He did graduate college but chose the jobs where he would have easy access to people with health conditions. As an orderly, he would not tell a nurse when a patient asked for a pain reliever. He would make the hospitalized wait hours before he would respond to a call, always saying I will be with you momentarily.

Then as a lab technician he found it so rewarding to jab the patient when drawing blood. As a physical therapist the readjustments he made for people would leave them shuddering in pain with the rough treatment.

This went on for years as he traveled from state to state and the various cities. It amused him that after he had worked in all 50 states, he started over again beginning with the first state and hospital where he had worked many years in the past.

Then finally one day all this caught up with him. By this time, he was an old man and needed to be hospitalized for his condition. He would never have guessed that there were others like him in the medical field.

As the orderly handled him roughly, he complained but it fell on deaf ears. He begged for sympathy and the orderly merely laughed at him and said, "Buddy you are out of luck." Those were the last words he heard as the pillow was placed over his face. His last thought was I know that face, he recognized his tormentor.

The Forensic Psychologist

She entered the room, expecting nothing from those that greeted her. A small woman, petite actually and outspoken. She speaks her mind. One of the women in the room found this woman's occupation fascinating as it involved counseling psychopaths. Upon learning this the questions flew from her interviewer. She had a definite response to each question put before her. She says she evaluates and then comes to a conclusion. She may prescribe a medication or suggest a plan for treatment. She adds that there are those that are pleasantly psychotic, yet they too can have a crisis.

She has suicides and has even been threatened by those that fear her and truthfully themselves. She reveals she works on contract with the state. She assesses and evaluates a criminal to judge whether an insanity plea is justified. She has had murderers and those that claim they did not do it which makes her job easier, she confides.

The cases are assigned and obviously, she cannot consult with someone she knows. As an example, she recounts that she went to school with one of the prisoners. She testifies in court, on Zoom, or sometimes the phone, to assist the judge to come to a conclusion.

When she has her first session for the day with a paranoiac, she was unconcerned for the most part though she realizes each case is different. This case however, proved to be difficult and frustrating.

She got no cooperation from Ben Simms and during the rather lengthy meeting, she confronted him about his lack of cooperation. Ben had killed his mother and sister, proclaiming it was in self-defense. She took no notice when he threatened her. It had happened before with others. The prison guard keeping an eye on the proceedings was unexpectedly called away on an emergency, she still felt no fear, confident that she was making progress with Ben. She could handle this yet no she couldn't.

Ben rose and approached her sadly yet suddenly placing his hands around her throat pressing the life out of her. Within three minutes she was extinguished. And when questioned, he simply said, "She was asking for it."

The Valley

She liked to use biblical names or aphorisms when texting that indicated or conveyed a "biblical" message. Rarely would she say, "When I can", she would say, "When I am able." Knowing the story of Cain and Able and by saying those few words she felt she was an Able. She often wondered what the ratio to Cains there were in the world.

Told by a psychologist years before not to read the Bible as it would confuse her, she took his patronizing words to heart and never did read the Bible, although for a time she collected them.

When she met a fellow named Luke, she asked his beliefs on good Samaritans. Did he believe they existed, or did they always have an underlying plan to benefit themselves? She liked to research Bible stories in order to work it into conversation but mostly emails or texts. She wanted to have it in writing.

This odd pastime was particularly ironic as she was an atheist but rarely shared that with others. When she did, she hoped for no judgement. During a time of torrential storms, she would ask her neighbor if he had started work on an ark. Or she would jokingly offer another fellow named Adam if he wanted a bite of her apple. Interestingly, she had a terrible fear of snakes but never related it to the Garden of Eden.

Her days turned into evenings, and time passed.

Listening in on a conversation between a young man and an elderly woman interested her, when the young man revealed timidly that he was a carpenter, and the lady smiled saying, "Jesus was a carpenter." Embarrassed, he did not reply but was obviously touched by her comment.

Anytime she noticed that a male colleague had gotten a haircut, she questioned if he was not afraid of losing his strength. The story of Samson and Delilah was beyond them as they would merely shrug their shoulders and return to work.

Then the months became years and as time passed she remembered when a friend had given her a book on the teachings of Christ. After some time, she inquired of her friend if she gave her the book because she was worried about her soul. Surprised her friend responded, "I have never been worried about your soul, I just wanted you to understand why people follow him." After this discussion, she often contemplated her mortality.

Years became decades and they too seemed to pass rapidly. At last, she lay dying, there were few friends with her, and they were genuinely surprised when she requested that someone read the 23rd Psalm to her from her King James Bible. And as she heard, "Though I walk through the valley of the shadow of death, I will fear no evil," she breathed her last.

Results

So far, the Russian Sage caught her attention. She wanted it in all its abundance in her garden. The owners of the house and garden were kind and had remodeled the house 12 years before. He had done nothing with the inherited house for years but then Sarah entered his life.

She was energetic and imaginative, and he liked all her ideas about their future together. They began their adventure riding a motorcycle throughout Arizona, New Mexico and California. They had their odd experiences which were small yet large, grand!! The first view of the Grand Canyon left such an impression that they swore to return.

After spending several months visiting most of California, they returned to the Grand Canyon, preparing to travel homeward once they had made one last visit to one of the seven wonders of the world. There were few people there on that sunny day and they were happy to be there together. When she proposed a final photo of the spectacular view they decided they would move on afterwards.

She suggested he back up a little farther to capture the shot. As he moved backward his ankle turned on a rock and pitched him over the edge. His cries of help left everyone in shock. To add to the dilemma, she threw herself toward him over the precipice saying. I must accompany him on this last voyage.

Unsolved Mystery*

Brazil has one of the world's highest rates of overall homicides. It ranks 3rd as a cause of death in Brazil.

The young Brazilian man was scrolling, looking for the news. "*Unsolved murder mystery,*" caught his eye. Miguel Flores decided to look into it further. They were called The Lead Mask Murders and there was a photo of two men in perforated metal masks covering their entire faces. Looking into it further, he discovered the men's names and as one was named Miguel he chose to continue to pursue the subject.

In searching, Miguel found that the claim that the tragedy was murder was erroneous. Sensationalism at its best. However, they did die under mysterious circumstances. Miguel found that the masks did not cover their entire faces, just the eyes. They were found lying side by side on a hilltop. It is believed that they both took a psychedelic while waiting to contact extraterrestrials.

The two electrical technicians were last seen August 17, 1966 and their bodies were discovered on August 20, 1966. Beside them was found a water bottle and a small notebook. The notebook revealed directions to be at a specified location at 16:30. They were to ingest capsules at 18:30. Both men were wearing waterproof coats. It is believed they were scientific spiritualists, and they were trying to contact other worlds. As they were exposed to the elements for 3 days, it was not possible to determine the actual case of death.

Another case of an unsolved mystery, Miguel thought and switched on the radio to hear more news of Rio de Janeiro.

* This is not fiction.

Unforeseen

Colleen was her name, and she looked as if she had stepped right out of the pages of Wuthering Heights. Pale, with black curls streaming down her back, she left quite an impression upon him at their first meeting. She, on the other hand, gave little thought to the fellow. It took several more encounters with him to be a blip on her radar.

It is not that she was haughty, quite the opposite. Often reticent in the company of others, she was aware of the looks she received. Was she searching for Heathcliff a dark and brooding soul or had she sworn off men finding them tiresome and at times rather thick. Their comments often left her cold and wishing she was elsewhere. Their attempts at flirtation bored her. She was in command of her emotions and showed little interest in adding drama into the mix. Her tendency to be aloof did not go unnoticed.

She was respected sometimes but more often ridiculed for her approach to life in society. Harsh words never crossed her mind in conversation, and she was generally pleasant yet very reserved and noncommittal when questioned about her opinions.

He wanted to draw her attention, for her to notice him. They walked daily for exercise and had chosen the same park to frequent. It could be a brisk walk of 1.2 miles, and they habitually would round the circle 5 times to achieve 6 miles. Sometimes she found they would be walking and pass one another several times.

It started with acknowledging one another with a slight nod of the head. After two weeks they began a verbal greeting and within a month he had asked her name, and they began to walk in the same direction.

He was quick-witted and made her laugh; however, he grew frustrated that she shared nothing about herself. He decided to ask her to have a coffee after their walk and she agreed hesitantly. All went well, and there was talk of going to dinner and a show one evening.

Seeing her at the loop the next day, he requested her number and said he would text her later that day. He seemed preoccupied and said little else parting suddenly.

As promised, he texted her and they made plans for the following Saturday night. She gave him her address, and he said he planned to be there by 7.

Arriving promptly, they got into his car and headed for the show planning to have a late dinner. She was talking animatedly to him for a change, and he was so enamored by her disclosures that he pulled out in traffic and was hit by a car going at an accelerated speed.

All of his top row of teeth were knocked out and she received 25 stitches in her face. They both recovered but never spoke again. There was no lesson learned here but the obvious, keep your eyes on the road.

From A Bottle

Robbie was what you would call "a good fellow." A man of few words, he was an enigma to the ones that knew him. He made a living doing research for an information supplier. All this fact-finding was done online, and he busied himself with following a pattern of research. He questioned what was the best manner in which to ask a question or avoid lengthy questions. These were just basic, practical approaches.

Although it was a solitary job, he had colleagues, and they shared research tips and sometimes a rare find. On seldom occasions they met up in-person, Robbie's mild manner and his personable demeanor was always pleasant to be around in a social setting.

The four researchers decided to rendezvous at a local pub to share some drinks and their day. Unaccustomed to alcohol, Robbie was feeling the effects of the two gin martinis he sampled when an inebriated, belligerent giant of a man threatened one of the four companions.

Suddenly, Robbie jumped upon the drunkards back and pummeled him soundly. The man slumped to the floor and the altercation ended. Robbie felt very drunk when he had done and was conscious that the archaic term pot-salience gave him the courage to fight the man as a result of intoxication.

Man's Best Friend

I did not know her well and do not remember what sparked the conversation we were having that inspired this disclosure. In her late 50s, she has a successful career and just generally tries to enjoy life. As I think about it, we were discussing deaths and how we chose to be laid to rest.

Obviously, there are few choices when it comes to internment or cremation. Not many wanted to be placed beneath the ground while most wanted cremation. I shared that I wanted to be sprinkled off the Second Street bridge in my hometown, when asked why, I merely responded because that is what I want.

In turn, I questioned her choice to which she never replied but then began the story of her father's death and his decision to be cremated. She continued with her declaration that she and her mother, once they received her father's ashes, decided to take the cremains into the heavily wooded area behind their house.
It was the favorite daily walking place for her father and his ever faithful dog, Chance. Chance had been raised and trained by her dad and even as a pup the loyal canine would follow him everywhere.

The dog became distraught that his master had seemingly disappeared. Chance whined, paced, and scratched at the door persistently but to no avail. Upon receiving the ashes, the two women walked into the wooded area and deposited the ashes in a narrow clearing in the forest. It was then that Chance appeared.

He ran directly to the pile of ashes and with a howl buried his face in his beloved friend's cremains.

The scene was tragic, and the mother and daughter had difficulty trying to discourage the dog's behavior. They gently pulled at his collar and finally were able to remove his muzzle from the cinders.

Each day the dog returns to the site until finally the wind dispersed the beloved friends cremains. Then one day as the daughter returned to the woods, she found Chance lying dead where he first discovered what had become of his best friend.

Widows

Statistically, women live longer than men. By age 85 women outnumber men by roughly 4 to 1. But who wants to live to be 85 you wonder? Research suggests that testosterone contributes to males' greater physical activity and aggressiveness and this "domino effect" leads to their higher death rate due to accidents and homicide.

Recent studies are revealing that women's death rate has increased in recent years because of having more stressful jobs and responsibilities whether by choice or life's determination.

Interestingly, the terms widow and widower comes from Old English in the feminine form a widuwe and less often used masculine form widuwa. She enjoyed reading this part. And found it encouraging.

Ashley was thinking of all this research she had done and admitted to herself that there was a reason for it. She wanted to outlive him and be able to dance on his grave. To her it would be the sweetest revenge.

Mortal Enhancers

This was a concept Elisabeth Wake and company were trying to sell. Her pitch to Sterling Overstreet consisted of reminding him that we all die. This is quickly followed with the persuasive approach that knowing this, the doomed should seek out pleasure and pursue their dream. Of course, she had no idea what his pursuit of pleasure would be. She only agreed to help him succeed, provided he sign on the dotted line. In doing so, he agreed to bequeath all his earthly possessions to the Mortal Enhancers Company if he should die in his quest for pleasure.

It did not take long for Sterling to feel that he would get the most pleasure out of competing in a horse race. He knew he was not Kentucky Derby material but thought he would be able to do some harness racing at the nearby track. Elisabeth agreed to finance this by paying for the horse, the sulky, and the horse harness. She had thoroughly checked Sterling's possessions and decided it was worth the investment. She was betting on his demise.

Sterling knew about the two types of harness racing, trotting and pacing. He chose pacing as 80% to 90% of harness racing is pacing. Pacing horses are faster and he was ready for the challenge. He trained daily and the time came to participate for a qualifier. He must finish the one-mile race in 2:04 or less in order to compete in the race set for 2 months in the future. The qualifier was scheduled for a week to the day from his inquiry.

The day came and his heart raced as he approached the horse and harness. He thought, with a chuckle, my heart is racing just as I will be in minutes. The pain traveled up his left arm to his heart and he gripped his chest as he fell to the ground dead. As Sterling did not die while actually racing, the company forfeited any rights to his estate.

What Luck!!

While playing solitaire on his phone, he noticed an ad at the bottom of the screen saying, "Play for cash." Hmm, he thought, I am not a gambler, but I am an awfully good solitaire player. Thinking that a chance to make some money was appealing and truthfully can't be a bad undertaking he decided to try his luck,

He was incredibly good or incredibly lucky and over time he managed to win upwards of $500. Feeling extremely fortunate he shared with his friends what he had been doing lately. They were impressed and urged him to try his luck in Las Vegas.

Acting what can only be considered rash, he mortgaged his inherited house, sold his car and made plans to fly out to Las Vegas from his midwestern hometown.

He researched what to expect and found that for one dollar a card or $52 he could play a game of solitaire against the house. He would receive $5 for each card in the "suit stack." The objective is to earn more points than is wagered. He made his plans, a stay at the Bellagio and to get gambling rights at the casino. Luck was definitely a lady that night as he exited through the doors $50,000 richer than when he entered.

As he strolled down the strip, he entered another casino in order to try the slot machines. He knew that millions could be won. He thought of the 92 year old retired grandmother from Illinois that won $22 million. This was the largest jackpot ever won by a woman in Las Vegas. His luck held and he would leave with $3 million.

As he walked outside to clear his mind and rejoice over his luck, he was amazed by the spectacular lightning and headed toward shelter to avoid the torrential thunderstorm. The lightning struck him as he retraced his steps. He had no time for a final fleeting thought, his death was instantaneous. The coroner wondered about this fellow's luck as only 20 people a year die from a lightning strike.

The Ruthless Relative

Quigley Morton was not a nice man, in fact, he was a cruel man. As a youth he tortured his pets until he was no longer allowed to have anything other than a goldfish bowl to which he added toilet bowl cleaner. His concerned parents were at a loss as to what to do with him.

As time passed, he grew to be a brutal adult. Both of his parents died before he reached the age of 21. The brother that he constantly tormented had distanced himself as much as possible from his brutish sibling. Orson Morton went on to have a good life; he married and was the father of two growing boys. Sadly, he too passed away before his sons were grown.

This is when Quigley stepped in. He told the grieving widow he would take one of his nephews to live with him to ease her financial worries and after some time she agreed, and her older son moved in with his uncle. At the time he was 16, naive and gullible.

They began to have problems almost immediately. Their relationship was doubly strained when the boy, Tyler, began bringing a girlfriend back to the small two-bedroom apartment. Quigley felt he had to get this kid out of his life. He remembered reading about a South Carolina nurse that had poisoned her husband with eyedrops. She claimed her innocence as well as her ignorance. She got away with it,

This sparked the idea as the perfect solution. Quigley decided to add a liberal amount of eye drops to Tyler's sandwich. When he made the purchase Quigley boasted to the pharmacy technician of his plan. Alarmed, the drugstore employee called the authorities to reveal the possibility of the uncle poisoning his nephew. The plan for Quigley was in place as he plotted to do this heinous deed the next day.

As he lay back in the bathtub's hot water, he stretched luxuriously and in doing so knocked Tyler's radio into the steaming bath. He was electrocuted. When the police arrived to question him, they had to break in the door, only to find Quigley's lifeless body floating in the tub. Tyler never returned to this scene and later he identified the body and curiously, to him, felt sadness.

A First

She was searching for firsts and discovered several firsts that rang true to her. She liked them, liked knowing that someone had these thoughts, wrote them and shared them with others.

She could relate to those that apologized first as the bravest, she was rarely one to apologize but when she did, it was heartfelt.

Also, acknowledging that those with short memories are the happiest was not a stretch for her as speaking truthfully to herself, she knew her memory was far too long and despised that she could dredge up memories, things she said, things said to her from many years in the past. She would often think I should have said this in response rather than saying nothing or something nonsensical.

And finally, the first to forgive is the strongest. These were what she considered transgressions that she found difficult to forgive. This was connected to her ego. How could or would someone say that to me? She is outraged and envisioned their deaths, for which she would have no sorrow.

All these firsts added up to a final decision to forget all this foolishness and just live her life and take things as they come. Overthinking would be her downfall, and she knew it.

Then as fate would have it, she saw him and all those thoughts came back, she remembered that she was never the one to apologize first, and that his memory was as good as her's so there would be no forgiveness.

They acknowledged one another briefly, and she wondered if he had a knowledge of the "the firsts." That was her question to him, and it inspired their conversation and impacted their future relationship of better understanding each other.

The Evangelistic Lifeguard

It was on the flight home, and the plane was nearly empty. She was going back to her hometown. She had been on a European tour, and this was the last leg of the journey.

She chose an aisle seat as she saw that the window seat was already filled. Then a man with sandy colored hair took the middle seat next to her and he began to talk.

He asked various questions, and it became apparent to her that he wanted to save her. It did not make her uncomfortable and she regarded him wryly. She rarely tells others that she is an atheist, she seeks to soften the claim with, "I am an agnostic." She decided telling him this would be a mistake.

He proceeded to tell her when he was a lifeguard aged 18, he saved a girl's life. He never revealed if this caused his spiritual transformation, or merely a Christian coincidence.

During the short flight from Chicago, he revealed that his wife was sitting across the aisle. The listener wondered if this was intentional. Either they wanted to have the opportunity to speak with other people or she just did not wish to listen to him.

The plane landed and he realized she was not someone he would be able to convert; they bid one another goodbye.

Spinach

All the guys called him Spinach because he was so green. The moniker seemed appropriate for someone like him. He was naive and kind with gentle eyes and a quiet voice.

Never one to be late, he hurried to the meeting place of some of his high school classmates. They asked him to join them at a chosen spot in the park. He complied with their wishes and hurried onward.

They had a surprise for him on this late fall day. Evenings were already becoming crisp and car windows glistened with light frost in the mornings. The plan was to show him the ropes, wake him up to reality. These cynical boys planned an ambush and to transport him to a tent in the woods and leave him there. He would have no idea where he was.

Word got around about what they had planned, and their scheme came to an end. The boys were bitter and never realized it was their bragging that brought their plan of action to an end.

In school Spinach gave a false bravado smile and went on about his days. Those days grew shorter, and the nights were colder. Autumn passed into winter with him growing accustomed to being jostled in the school's hallways and obscene notes pasted to his locker door.

He never attended the Friday night football games and preferred reading in solitude. He was currently reading D.H. Lawrences 1920 novel, Women in Love.

Upon finishing the novel, he found the film which was released in the U.S. January 1, 1969. The book and film changed his life and his attitude. He no longer dreaded the daily confrontations at school. He faced them with a quiet resolve.

Carefully watching the evening weather forecast, he learned that the night would bring snow and record-breaking freezing temperatures. Perfect for his plan. At midnight, he crept from his parents' house and walked into the cold in his pajamas and bare feet.

They found him the next morning, just as they found the actor Oliver Reed in the film, frozen to death. He had researched that freezing is painless, those were his last thoughts as he slipped into unconsciousness.

In Flight

She was assigned to the middle seat and felt neither disappointment nor enthusiasm. Seating herself first, a man stood waiting to be allowed access to the window seat. A woman arrived and took the aisle seat.

As this was an international flight, she settled and told herself, make the best of this. Drifting off to sleep took no time as her head rested gently onto her chest. It was then that the dreams began.

These were what you would call disturbing dreams, ones to which she could find no reason. The first dream was vivid and terrifying.

Seeing through the eyes of a man with his hands around the victim's throat squeezing the life out of her. Breathless, she awoke in fear. The passenger on the aisle was regarding her questioningly.

Once again, she closed her eyes, and the dreams resumed. This time her slumber was deep, and her head fell back against the seat, mouth open. She was a mouth breather.

The dream was chaotic and involved many unknown faces, all leering at her and laughing. Again, this awakened her abruptly. Uncomfortable, she tried to readjust her seat, unsuccessfully. The remainder of the trip was uneventful; however, she still had an uneasy feeling. Once landed, the aisle cleared quickly, and the man seated next to her followed her out of the plane's main cabin.

To her surprise, there were some very serious looking men, watching as the flight's passengers filed out. They made a move for the man behind her; he grabbed her to use her as a shield.

This all seemed so familiar, and she realized, it was all in her dreams.